Space Dog Alfred

The Professor was dying. He knew that. He knew that the project American billionaire Hiram T Filibuster had given him could not now be completed. Well it wouldn't be completed by him anyway.

"What are we going to do, Alfred?"

Alfred didn't say anything but he lay down and looked at the Professor with those big sad brown eyes and that was enough.

"You see, Alfred. The space ship is complete. I have run all the tests and it is ready to take me through space to amazing unknown planets. The thing is, Alfred, I can't go. I am too ill for the journey now."

Just then Tom and Seren, the Professor's grandchildren, the twins, came bursting into the room full of life and enthusiasm. They were just what the Professor needed. He winced as Seren bounced on the bed but he wasn't really angry.

"How are things today, Prof?"

They loved calling him 'Prof'. They were proud of having a grandfather who was a professor. He got his professorship from the website of the University of Lunology. They gave it to him for his work on capturing moonlight and putting it in to night lights. He had paid the University ten dollars for a certificate of professorship.

The moonlight into night light idea had not quite worked but the millionaire, Hiram T Filibuster had been so impressed with the professor's idea, that he had donated millions of pounds towards the space ship.

"Do you want some tea?" Seren knew the answer to that and went straight away to make the professor's tea. She used a special pot of the prof's own devising which had two spouts. As he only used one cup there was always a certain amount of waste.

The prof always had his tea made from shredded newspaper and boiling water. He liked to use the *Daily Telegraph* because the ink ran nicely and it saved him having to read it. Mixed with milk and several spoonfuls of sugar he said it tasted delicious but he could never persuade anyone else to try it. He realised his taste was a little eccentric.

Alfred thought it was barking. He was far too polite to say and besides he was a dog and dog's can only talk in stories. Excuse me a minute.

Ah. Well I've just had a discussion with my editor and she reminded me this **is** a story. Alfred, as I say, could not talk of course. What he could do was to transmit his thoughts. The professor's brain was always so full of ideas that there was no chance for Alfred to get through to him. Tom and Seren however had a thought from Alfred and they acted on it immediately.

"What are you unhappy about Prof?"

"Well it's this wretched illness. I seem to get weaker and weaker. I have worked night and day on the space ship Hiram T Filibuster sponsored and it is now ready to go. I just don't think I can make it now. If only there were someone..." he trailed off and looked at Seren and Tom thoughtfully.

"We would do anything to help." thought Alfred.

"Yes we would do anything to help." They both said.

"But you are too young. I couldn't let you take the risk of going alone."

"Well take me then." thought Alfred.

"Well take me then." said Tom and wondered what he was talking about.

"I think he means take Alfred," said Seren.

"You need another pair of hands I would have thought. Not paws." said the Prof.

"Well, we could always ask Uncle Finn."

"Uncle Finn, that old rascal." The prof chuckled. He had a soft spot for Finbar Cool and in the end the twins persuaded him to talk to Finn about it.

"Seren, we're going into space!" Tom exclaimed.

"Is stating the obvious your chosen subject."

They both laughed.

Finbar Cool

Uncle Finn was a dealer but nobody could tell you from day to day what he was dealing in. When asked he always said he was selling fridges to Eskimos. He had a shop but his shop was a suitcase. He often had it resting on the boot of his car in case he had to make a quick getaway.

"Now ladies, you can see bracelets almost the same as this in the shops in the high street. They cost twenty five pounds. Mine are just the same. The only difference is that theirs come in by the front door and mine go out by the back door.

"I am not asking you for twenty pounds. I am not even asking you for ten pounds. Five pounds that's all I want. I am robbing myself."

"Well that would make a change," said one of the women gathered around him and the others laughed..

"Come on, Finn," another asked, "why not tell us where you got them from?"

"Now then Mary. I am not asking you where you got the five pounds from am I? Hello hello hello, who's this? It's the terrible twins."

Tom and Seren had heard Uncle Finn selling before. Half of what he said was nonsense. The other half was rubbish. People still bought his stuff though.

Seren always kicked him in the shins when he called them 'the terrible twins" which may have been why he did it.

"Ah Ah me war wound. She's trying to kill me." Finn was hopping about. People always gathered around him when he was selling. It was as good as a pantomime.

"Uncle Finn," Seren began when he had finished clowning, "the prof wants to see you."

"Well I will pop round for tea later if that is OK with his Professorship. On second thoughts I will be bringing my own tea. Listen can you do me a favour in return?"

"What might that be?"

"Well can you sort-of keep a look out for the rozzers?"

"The who?"

"Now you know very well what I mean: the filth, the fuzz, the bluebottles, the coppers, the Old Bill."

Seren and Tom continued to look blank. They had played this game before.

"The police," Uncle Finn sighed, "I don't know what they teach you at school, I really don't. I want you two to let me know if you see them coming from either direction. There will probably be an ice-cream in it for you later."

"What flavour?" Seren asked.

"Any flavour you like, Princess."

"So one minute I'm a terrible twin and the next minute I'm a Princess?"

"Well if you do me this favour you will be."

"What about me?" asked Tom.

"Well you will be a prince obviously, your royal highness." The women laughed to see Finn bowing low to Tom and Seren.

Later that day, Tom and Seren were playing "Attack of the Mutant Zombies." when Uncle Finn crept up on them.

He made the sort of noise he thought a mutant zombie would make. He made it loud enough to make them jump out of their skins and then laugh hysterically.

"Well I only hope there are no mutant zombies on any of the planets we are going to be visiting."

"You mean..."

"Yes I do mean. You guys and me. We are heading for the stars."

"Wow this is terrific."

"OK Seren there is no need to try and hug me to death."

"So it will just be the four of us: You, us and Alfred. Alfred the Space Dog!"

"Yes. I have some good news for you. It will be five of us. Abby is coming too!"

"Oh that's terrific!" shouted Tom.

"Yes that's terrific." said Seren. And she tried hard to make it sound as if she meant it. Abby was their cousin. She was the same age and size as Seren and Seren suspected her of taking her clothes and make-up when she stayed at their house. Abby had a sweet smile which always convinced Tom of her innocence and Uncle Finn was all for peace whatever the rights or wrongs of things.

Five go to the stars

The space ship was completely round like a golf ball and it was smooth and black. There was no doorway that they could see but they each had a remote, except for Alfred. They practised opening and closing the doors while they were waiting for Hiram T Filibuster to arrive.

"Why is it round?" asked Abby.

"It is the way to get the biggest amount of room inside." said Tom. Tom liked explaining things. He especially liked explaining things to Abby.

Hiram T Filibuster had been flown over from America in his private jet. On the ground he went everywhere on a specially adapted scooter. When they saw him they thought he looked the same shape as the spaceship.

Mr Filibuster's manservant broke a bottle of root beer against the titanium hull of the ship. Hiram T Filibuster never touched alcohol. "I name this ship the Hiram T Filibuster. God bless her and all who fly to the stars in her. I am only sorry that the man who has made this all possible, Professor Farnsbarns, is unable to be with us for this important event."

Hiram T Filibuster then said the same thing in slightly different words and to finish off he said it all again. By now he was sweating.

They had a last meal together in the local branch of Filibuster Burgers. Hiram T Filibuster had a double Filibuster with extra cheese then followed it up with another. "Best food in the world." He said between mouthfuls. "Best food in the world. Best food in the world."

It seemed he had to say everything at least three times. He followed this up with a burp which had the staff rushing out of the kitchen to see what was going on.

"He's going to repeat that twice now." said Uncle Finn and the children laughed quietly so he wouldn't hear. They need not have worried. Hiram T Filibuster only ever heard the sound of his own voice.

Uncle Finn noticed that the non-drinker had a little flask in his inside pocket and he took a little drink from it now and again.

Hiram T Filibuster saw Uncle Finn looking and said quickly, "It's medicine. Medicine. It's medicine."

Uncle Finn reached out his hand and said he would like to try that medicine. He took a big swig and started coughing.

"It really is medicine!"

Hiram T Filibuster smiled.

When they had all had as much Filibuster as they could stomach, it was time to get on the ship.

"Embark." said Tom importantly.

"No, Alfred hardly ever barks." Seren answered.

"It means get on the ship."

"Well we could just say 'get on the ship.'" said Seren.

The Prof had made a video to explain about the ship.

To begin with they had a picture of his bedside table and a voice in the background saying,

"Now. Oh. Is this microphone working? Well I think I will just move the camera a bit. That's better. Right. Now I am ready to start. The Hiram T Filibuster is completely automatic. You will not notice the take-off. In fact, you will now have taken off. You see, you didn't notice it did you?

"The ship will travel faster than light and if you are not strapped in you will find yourselves floating about a lot because you will be weightless."

There was a short panic as everyone strapped themselves in before they floated out of their chairs. Alfred even had a strap on his dog basket. The prof didn't want him injured.

"The ship will be searching among the stars for planets. Tom will tell you at length about the difference between planets and stars. Basically you can live on a planet but I wouldn't try living on a star. It is looking for planets in the Goldilocks zone.

"Who's been eating my porridge?" said Finn and they had to rewind because they had laughed over the next bit.

"This is the rather silly name given to the zone where planets are not too hot for life and not too cold. They are "just right" like baby bear's porridge. These planets may have life. You are to find out about it. The ship will land automatically. There is a manual override so you can take control of the ship at any time. DO NOT TOUCH IT!

"Now I suggest you have a go at moving around in zero gravity. I won't be able to talk to you again because a phone call would take at least ten years to get through at the speed of light. I have left some DVDs which you can watch which give more information. I have tried to answer any question you may have. Now good luck and God bless."

At first they were very careful about moving in zero gravity. At first they held on to all the hand-holds which the professor had put all round the walls. Then Tom realised how much fun it could be and he started crossing the cabin space and bouncing off the walls.

"I wonder if that is a good idea, Tom." was all that Uncle Finn said about it.

Then Tom was violently sick. He was sick upwards and downwards and sideways at the same time. Uncle Finn gave him a plastic bag to collect it all up with and he was a bit more careful from then onwards.

As time went by they got over the effect of what they called the Filibuster Fat-burgers and tried the food. All of the food was in tubes.

"It is a bit like eating toothpaste," said Abby

"Yes. Except the toothpaste tastes better." said Seren.

There was no day and night here but the lights dimmed for eight hours and they tried to sleep strapped to their bunks. In the end they got so used to it that when they got to a planet they found the gravity seemed strange.

Then there came a day when the shipboard computer rang an alarm and the one word "Planetfall." Like Hiram T Filibuster, it repeated it twice more.

Planetfall

The next thing that happened was another video from The Prof

"You have arrived at a new planet. You will be able to replay this video at any time but it will not play every time you reach a new planet.

"The remotes you all have will link you to the ship's computer to provide a translation service. You need to get the inhabitants of the planet to talk to you so the computer can work out their language.

"They may look strange but it is likely there is intelligent life on this planet. Do not think of them as "aliens". It is unhelpful. Good luck."

"Well we are already used to strange looking creatures, eh Alfred?" said Uncle Finn.

Alfred took this in his stride. That was not because he did not know what Uncle Finn was saying. Alfred did understand every word said to him He had learned not to take offence if people didn't like the way he looked.

"What kind of a dog is he?" asked Abby

"Well he's a French Bulldog. It's a cross-breed." said Tom, who knew everything.

"What a cross between a dog and a bat?" Abby continued, stroking one of Alfred's large pointed ears.

"Well a cross between a pug and a Bulldog and now you mention it, probably a bat as well." Tom said, "Now where on earth is Seren?"

"Well, I don't know how to tell you," Finn put in, "but she is not on earth at all. Neither are you. Here she comes."

Seren is one of those people who go red when they are angry. She was quite red now.

"Have any of you seen my red top? The one with the Aztec stitching."

"You must have lost it somewhere. We are about to see the light of an alien sun on a completely new planet. It is the biggest adventure ever. Can we worry about the top later?" Tom was keen to get out there.

"Have you seen it?" Seren asked Abby.

Abby just smiled.

"Come on," Uncle Finn was unusually businesslike, "I will help you look for it when we come back. Now we really must get on."

They opened the double doors and the bright light of the planet's sun was let in. They paused, realising what an important moment this was.

"One small step for man..." Uncle Finn started.

"And one big playground for a dog!" Seren interrupted as Alfred bounded out into the sunlight. They followed him into what they thought was the grass. Seren was the first to notice.

"Oh no! This isn't grass at all."

They all looked down. It most certainly was not grass. It was about a centimetre high and it was all white, pure white. There were glimpses of something red through the white.

"It...it's more like fur than grass." Seren knelt down to touch it. She found herself stroking it. "It's warm. It's as if it were alive."

Uncle Finn didn't find this frightening. In fact nothing frightened Uncle Finn. He cupped his hands around his mouth and shouted "Take us to your leader!" so loud it made the others jump and then laugh. They laughed rather loud to show they were not afraid.

Ahead of them were what looked like trees but they were of many colours, red, orange, brown, white and perhaps strangest of all, purple.

Tom was uneasy suddenly. He got the idea that someone, the trees themselves perhaps, was listening to them. He didn't like it at all.

Alfred could feel that Tom felt threatened by something from the trees and he ran towards them and adopted a fighting stanoc with his front legs stiff and his shoulders up. He let out the unearthly whining howl which a French Bulldog will make when he feels threatened by anything.

The others were taken aback by Alfred's behaviour. They were even more taken aback when they heard a similar howl coming back from the trees!

Alfred was not a dog to retreat. It was not in his nature. Big as these trees were, they would have to come through him if they meant any harm to the humans.

"It's just an echo." Finn laughed and then he tried shouting "echo!" to see if the woods would do it again.

Nothing happened. It was the same when the others tried. Alfred didn't howl again. Once was enough.

"Right I think we need to go south." Finn said pointing towards the trees.

"What do you mean south? We don't know where south is on this planet." Tom said. He was about to go on at length about the earth's magnetic core when Finn explained.

"I got this mobile phone for a hundred pounds, though I could let you have a very similar one for fifty pounds. Before we left earth I downloaded an app to navigate on an alien planet. I think the Prof was responsible for writing it.

"As far as my phone is concerned the ship is always north. So any direction we go in from the ship is south. Those trees, if they are trees, are to the south of us."

He got out the phone to show them. There was an arrow pointing back towards the ship and they found that it went on pointing in that direction wherever they moved it.

"I can't get text messages on it but then, you see, I never did read them because I'm Dis-clectic, disprexic... you know I can't tell my aunt from my elbow when I'm reading. Come on. Forward troops."

"You know I think we ought to have brought guns, ray guns or something." Tom said. He was getting scared again as they approached the trees. The others were getting a bit scared too.

They noticed that what they thought of as trees looked as if they were all one plant with trunks of many colours connected by what looked like branches which seemed to grow from different trunks and intertwine.

"Well, Major Tom, I remind you that it is illegal to export guns to another planet, you know. I might have one tucked away somewhere I will have to have a look. Meanwhile I have got knives." Uncle Finn said as he unhitched his rucksack and pulled something out to give to Tom.

"That isn't a knife!" Tom protested,

Finn looked at it. "You know you're right, young Tom. It is a corkscrew.. Hold on to it will you. I bet you could do some damage to a tree that misbehaved with that."

He fumbled in the bag and brought out a set of vicious-looking knives and let Tom have his pick. Seren and Abby were not all that keen on having a knife so Finn said he would look after theirs for the time being.

As they got close to the trees they saw there were gaps in the plant of many trees where they could enter. They hadn't been able to see them before. In fact it seemed as if there had never been any gaps but they had opened up as they were approaching.

Alfred led the way. He was followed by Finn who feared nothing. Abby followed her dad. Seren and Tom looked at each other and shrugged. They weren't going to be shamed by the others going where they feared to go. They went under the shadow of the plant.

They walked bravely into the tree or trees.

"What should we call it?" asked Abby.

"Well the tree monster is one idea or the tree of a kind." said Uncle Finn

"Or just the wood." suggested Seren practically.

"Mmm that depends on whether it *is* wood." Tom was touching a tree.

The others touched the trunk nearest to them. It felt like something they could almost remember. The most powerful thought in their minds was that they should join hands and become part of whatever it was.

"No no no." Uncle Finn wasn't having that, "Are you all thinking what I'm thinking? That we should become part of the wood? Well that idea isn't coming from us. We never think the same, do we?"

"No." They all took their hands away from the wood and the idea faded but it was still there lurking behind the back of their minds, ready to come out again when the time was right.

They followed the path the wood seemed to be guiding them along. They came to a clearing covered with the short white fur they had seen before. In the clearing there was a figure.

They couldn't be quite clear what colour the figure was.

"It looks green to me." Tom was very definite.

"It looks blue to me." Seren insisted.

"It looks like mauve or perhaps indigo." offered Abby

"Or perhaps it looks red like that famous top of yours!" she whispered so only Seren could hear.

They all knew Uncle Finn was colour-blind. "I can't tell my colours from my whites. And I get my murds wuddled as well."

What they all did see was that the figure raised a hand and the wood parted to invite them into the clearing.

She was, as Tom later said, an ordinary girl. Except for the fact she was green and about half their height. Little details like that. "And talking of details there was de tail." Finn insisted on adding.

She did indeed have a tail which may or may not have been green.

She looked at Alfred seriously. Then to their surprise, she went down on all fours, looked him right in the eye and gave a wailing howl. She tried to stiffen her arms and look as much like a French Bulldog as possible.

Alfred realised she had picked him as the leader of the party because he was the most intelligent. He needed to get one of the humans to speak for him.

He tried directing his thoughts at Uncle Finn, he wasn't really his uncle but he was prepared to allow him to lead.

Uncle Finn's mind was elsewhere however.

Alfred tried Tom and Seren.

"Uncle Finn," Seren said in her most winning voice, "the silly thing thinks Alfred is our leader.

"And it would be best if you spoke on Alfred's behalf."

Uncle Finn wasn't going down on all fours, not at his age. Instead he held his head high and said,

"I am Finbar McBridey O'Shaughnessy the third." He was making it up as he went along. His surname was Cool. I am speaking on behalf of Lord Alfred er Tennyson here."

He patted Alfred on the head.

The girl made some noises. Uncle Finn continued. "We are travellers from a distant star and we have come seeking your planet er from the sky. He added that because he had an idea that telling her about the ship might be a bad idea.

The girl made some more noises and looked at Uncle Finn. By now the translator had something to go on and it said, "Why cannot I speak to your leader?"

"Damn it girl I am the..." Finn decided this was not the way to go. Instead he said to the translator, "The Lord Alfred does not speak to you but I am his talker." The noises coming out of the translator were at least as strange as the noises Alfred made when he was threatened but they supposed they would get used to it.

"Where are we? What is this place called?"

"The earth." was the surprising reply.

"Finbar McBridey O'Shaughnessy. You seem very surprised." The girl said with a hint of a smile on her face. She seemed amused

"Well it's just that we come from there."

"So do we." she said quite reasonably.

"But we are billions of, trillions of...just a very long way away." Uncle Finn protested.

"And you call your planet 'The Earth'. Now that is quaint." The girl said in a condescending tone

Uncle Finn was so flummoxed by this he didn't notice they had not been using the translator. The girl was talking English now. The others did notice. They gathered round her with lots of questions.

"What is your name?"

"How old are you?"

"What colour are you exactly?"

She looked at them in silence for a while and then said, "It changes with the light. Colours change with the light. You must have noticed.

"I have been alive for 50 rotations of the earth around the star – you will have to do the Maths yourselves.

"And names? What is in a name?"

They introduced themselves anyway. They said they came in peace.

"What is peace, please?"

"Well." Tom thought about that one. It meant the absence of war but she might have no experience of war, the lucky devil. "It means friendship." He held out his hand. She looked at it. Then she frowned a little.

Then Tom shook hands with Uncle Finn. Catching on, Uncle Finn shook hands with the three others and then knelt down and shook hands with Alfred. When everyone had shaken hands with everyone else and the 120 handshakes were completed, he held his hand out to the girl and said, "how do you do?"

She solemnly shook hands with Alfred. Then she looked at Finn and said, "How do I do what?"

He decided this was a useless course of discussion so he opted for:

"What is your name?"

"Name?"

"Well my name is Finn. This is Tom. This is Seren. This is Abby. This is Alfred."

"Well Finn is shorter than Finbar McBridey O'Shaughnessy the third anyway. You can call me Ardin."

"Can you tell us the name for the tree, Ardin?" Uncle Finn swept his hand around the glade."

"Tree. You can call her Gai."

"Guy?" said Uncle Finn, "I can only say she is one Hell of a Guy."

"We have to go and make a report to Hiram T Filibuster on the radio (He wont get it for ten years. I don't think the Prof explained that bit to him though). We would like to return here to speak with you tomorrow."

"You cannot return here," said Ardin firmly.

"Why not?"

"You cannot return because you cannot leave. You have seen the sacred glade. You cannot leave."

They noticed that Gai seemed to close in on itself so that there was no way for them to escape from the glade.

Abby, infuriated at the trap, made a grab for Ardin. Ardin just laughed and changed colour rapidly as she slipped away so they couldn't see where she was.

Suddenly a gap opened in Gai and closed. They heard Ardin's voice from beyond the tree.

"I will see you again tomorrow. If you survive the night."

"She seems to be a very powerful young lady," Finn mused, "It is a mistake to judge how powerful someone is from their size. She is more like a leprechaun or an elf than anything else. Yet she has power over Gai who is much much bigger. She might almost be the national elf."

For once one of Finn's jokes fell flat. He decided to lighten the mood, and the glade which was rapidly getting dark, by producing some lamps from his pack and some food. The food was mainly tubes such as they had on the ship but he also had some sweets which looked like the branded sweets in the shops but weren't. Much cheaper but just as good, as Uncle Finn always said.

Nightfall was very sudden. A few minutes after Ardin left the sacred glade it would have been pitch dark but for the light of Uncle Finn's two lamps. "The batteries are recharged by solar power. We can't buy batteries here and we can't buy oil for lamps but the light of this star will do as well as solar power." Uncle Finn explained.

There were no stars.

"How can there be no stars?" asked Seren.

"Dark matter," Tom said darkly. "You can't see all the stars at home. There are an infinite number. The sky would be all silver at night. The gaps are dark matter. There must be an awful lot of it around this Earth."

Soon the moon rose. It was not almost circular like the earth moon. It was smaller, it moved faster and it was oval.

"You know that might just be the oddest thing I've seen. I thought all moons were round, like the earth's moon." said Abby

"Oh no," said Tom who knew everything, "Phobos and Deimos, the moons of Mars are really irregular shapes. They are named after the sons of Mars who signified the horror and terror of war."

"Funny the Romans knew horror and terror were the sons of war and then went on making war all the time." was Seren's comment.

"You know, I visited a planet where nothing ever happened." Uncle Finn decided it was time for one of his stories. "There was no time. There were no days, hours or minutes and everyone was bored from morning to night."

"When did you visit this planet?" asked Abby.

"I just told you there was no time there. So I couldn't visit it at a particular time."

"How could everybody be bored? If nothing changed there couldn't be any people." Tom tried to be logical. This was never a good idea with Uncle Finn.

"Well there were no people of course. I was bored. And since I was the only person there, well surely I was everyone."

At that point, Alfred howled in the general direction of the moon. The moon itself had vanished and it was suddenly even darker in the sacred glade. Then the moon reappeared.

They watched in horror as a great chunk of the moon vanished again.

"That looked like a wing." said Tom.

"I think you have the right of it, Major Tom. But a bird that big! Can you hear me Major Tom, it must be enormous." said Uncle Finn

"Look," said Seren, "there must be more than one of them."

There was another giant wing obscuring part of the moon.

They felt the draught as one of the giant birds or bats came close to them but they could see nothing clearly.

"That was frightening." Finn admitted, although he didn't seem frightened himself until suddenly Seren shouted out "Where is Abby?"

They searched the sacred glade with torches but there was no sign of Abby. They were all thinking that the giant bat must have taken Abby but none of them were saying it.

Alfred was thinking that Abby was the one who had made a grab for Ardin. Could Ardin have sent the giant bat to teach Abby a lesson? If so, Abby would live, because a lesson was no use to a dead girl.

What the Veck?

It was neither a bat nor a bird. The hands that were gripping Abby were like human hands but huge. And the Veck (they were called Veck) could speak. It was speaking now.

"Calm down, dear. You've just been kidnapped on an alien planet by a giant flying creature. What is there to worry about?"

When she could say anything, the first thing that came to mind wasn't "who, what or why" but "You can speak English!"

"Ardin taught us. We are quick learners. Ah here we are."

With that they landed in a high mountain cave where a number of Veck lived. He took off his wings and stored them carefully. The cave, Abby soon found out, was filthy. There were three Veck there and no toilet or waste bin in sight. It was a mess.

"What is your name?"

"Abby. What is yours?"

"We don't have names. We are the Veck. We all think the same and we all look the same so there is no point in having names."

"What is going on?"

"I can't answer that," said the Veck. If they could smile, he would have been smiling. "So many things are going on. The earth is going round the star. I am breathing. The first moon is about to set. Some strangers have entered the sacred glade for the first time ever. The list goes on and on."

"Why have you kidnapped me?"

"Look around you. Isn't it obvious? We kidnapped you because we need a cleaner. Nobody on earth will come up here and clean for us. You will have to do."

"Will I ever see my family again?"

"We are your family now."

Abby cried. The Veck waited patiently until she had quite finished. Abby pleaded but the

Veck was deaf to her pleas.

"Look, perhaps if I am a very good cleaner you will listen to me then."

"Well I haven't seen any cleaning from you yet."

"Well is there a broom?"

"What is a broom?"

It dawned on Abby that she was going to have to clean this stinking cave with her bare hands. She cried again.

While she was crying the Veck went to the back of the cave and came back with the most evil-smelling rag you can imagine. In fact you probably can't imagine how disgusting it was. Just imagine a cloth which has cleaned out a filthy cave full of every kind of smelly mess and has never been washed out. It was pretty awful.

"This is the filth cloth." he said, offering it to her. Abby didn't want to touch it so he dropped it at her feet.

"Now get on with it!"

The Veck watched as Abby began to try to clean the filthy cave with the filth cloth.

She found that the cave was full of things the Veck had just picked up and brought there and lost interest in. In the darkness at the back of the cave she stumbled on some fibres like willow. This gave her an idea.

While they slept, and they slept a lot, she started weaving a basket. She had done this at school a few times and this stuff, whatever it was, was very like willow although it was blue. When she had completed it, she showed it to the Veck. They reacted as if she had done something magical. The Veck were proud of the fact that they never made anything except a mess.

They passed the basket from hand to hand and marvelled at it.

One asked, "Very nice, but what is it for?"

"It is called a rubbish basket. You put rubbish in it."

"Why would we do that?"

"It makes it easier to keep the cave clean."

"Yes it is a very nice rubbish basket." Then they went back to playing a game which was a bit like dice, except their dice had seven sides.

They were not so pleased when they found Abby nagging them every time they dropped something on the nice clean cave floor.

"I just cleaned this floor. You can't put rubbish on it. I have made a lovely rubbish bin. You put the rubbish in the rubbish bin. Look, Veck, there is a lovely new basket. You admired it when I showed it to you. It is called a rubbish basket. There is a clue in the name. You put rubbish in it. You do not put the rubbish on the floor. Do you understand?"

"Well you are supposed to pick up the rubbish. Just pick it up and put it in the bin."

"You put it in the bin."

"No you put it in the bin."

"What did your last servant die of?"

The Veck thought about it for a moment and said, "Asking questions."

If he thought this would shut Abby up, he didn't know Abby.

Every time any of them put rubbish on the floor they got the same speech. Abby got more and more sarcastic with them. Eventually they started putting rubbish in the bin. Abby was delighted.

One day, one of the Veck said to her, "You asked me once what our last cleaner died of."

"Yes."

"Well he was a gnarl, if you know what I mean. A nasty little creature which does not share our mind. It may have a mind of its own. I don't know. Anyway this particular gnarl had been captured in a raid. The gnarl like to steal and they had stolen an animal we intended to hunt. So instead we hunted them and captured this little fellow.

"He was not a good cleaner. He was not like you with your basket. The gnarl cannot fly of course. They live most of the time underground. One day everyone was out and the gnarl took it into his mind to steal a pair of wings. As far as we know he launched himself from the cave mouth. All we ever found found was a broken pair of wings and a very broken gnarl at the bottom of the mountain.

"That is sad." said Abby.

"No. We have you to clean now and one less gnarl is one less thief in the world."

"That seems heartless, " Abby protested.

"What is heartless? I have a heart. It pumps the blood around and all that sort of thing. No you are quite wrong about that. Now get back to cleaning, Abby."

Abby had all sorts of ideas in her mind after that. She thought about escaping, since nobody had tried to rescue her. She thought about the poor gnarl and how it had made a brave attempt to get away. And she thought about the food. The Veck used to catch and eat animals. The diet was raw meat. She was a vegetarian normally and raw meat was pretty disgusting. All she got was the bits the Veck couldn't be bothered to eat. She ate table scraps of fat and gristle while she was cleaning up.

She had a firm intention to escape. The only question was "How?"

Alfred the Great

The humans had searched the glade a hundred times. They had tried calling Abby's name. Alfred had dutifully gone around sniffing as if he were a bloodhound. He could hear Abby's thoughts but they were miles away and very unhappy. The flying creatures had obviously kept her alive but he couldn't reassure the humans much.

He sent the thought to Tom and Seren "I am sure she is all right." and Finn had agreed. Finn thought she was definitely not all right but saw no point in frightening Tom and Seren. After all any of them might be next to go.

The night seemed to last for ages. The second moon came up. It was even more irregular than the first. It looked like a sugar cube that someone had given a good suck. They were not to know that this moon was called the "herald of the dawn" on this Earth and daylight would only be half an hour away.

They tried attacking Gai but this was in vain. The corkscrew and even the most ugly-looking knife in Uncle Finn's pack could make no impression on it. It seemed to be harder than iron. Worse, they felt as soon as the knife touched Gai the idea which was lurking behind their minds came forward. They felt that they needed to join Gai and become part of it.

Alfred sat and he thought. For a while he did complicated long-division sums to calm his mind. Then he thought about the problem they really faced. They were trapped within the sacred glade. They could not escape. They did not know where Abby was. They did not know who had taken her. They did not know how to rescue her. They had a bit of food but soon they would starve.

There were no gaps in the forest Gai had created around them. They could not attack Gai because Gai was too strong. They could only talk to Gai through Ardin. Just a minute. Who said they could only contact Gai through talking to Ardin?

In moments Alfred had come up with the answer. They needed to contact Gai themselves.

Gai

Alfred began the strangest journey possible by simply walking across the glade and touching his nose to Gai. There was an overwhelming feeling that he had to join Gai and become part of her. He wanted to get away from this monster but he deliberately pushed forward. Gai opened up to accept him and suddenly he was really inside a new colourful world.

Alfred was completely colour-blind but having the power of Gai all around him was overwhelming. He could see some strange horrible alien creatures, three of them, searching the sacred glade. He realised that he was seeing Uncle Finn, Tom and Seren through Gai's eyes. Gai was interested in them but did not see them as much of a threat.

He looked around, fascinated by the power of Gai's vision. The roots went into the tunnels of the gnarl. Gai focussed on the ground and then delved further. He could see (and hear and smell and feel) the gnarl in their underground homes. The gnarl were a dark browny green. Alfred realised that Gai was not colour-blind. On the contrary, Gai loved colour.

The gnarl were constantly busy. The Veck never worked. They slept and they hunted. For them hunting was a kind of play.

As he watched them, it seemed that the gnarl never stopped. Some were washing, scrubbing floors and cleaning and polishing machines in vast underground workshops. The noise of the machines was deafening. Others were mining, forging, lifting and carrying. He could see that they were collecting what looked like weapons, hammers and blades in a gigantic cave. The cave was lit by lanterns the gnarl had made from what looked like skulls lit from within with a red light. The walls were dripping with water. The red light glinted on the weapons and made it look as if they were edged with blood.

Their talk showed that they were preparing for war. Gai definitely saw them as a serious threat. Alfred saw them as a threat too now. He was becoming more and more a part of Gai. He was in danger of losing himself.

He tried to reach out to Abby's mind and he could see a cave with a spectacular view over the land and he saw the nasty little habits of the Veck. He couldn't believe how filthy the cave was. He had never seen Abby working before either. On the ship all she did was lounge around playing video games or sneak into Seren's room when she thought nobody could see her. He could see that she was unhappy but alive and well.

In the glade, Tom awoke from a light sleep and found himself drawn towards the tree. He touched it for a moment and closed his eyes. He went straight to Uncle Finn and grabbed his foot. This was a way of waking him up that always worked.

"Wha..."

"I have touched the tree."

"I warned you about that." said Uncle Finn who was now fully awake.

"I got a message. Alfred is safe and well and he has become a part of Gai. Gai says that Abby is safe and not a part of Gai. Gai cannot lie."

"Gai cannot lie? Well it rhymes but how do we know?"

"It is just a feeling but if you were to touch Gai..." Tom started

"Not on your life!" Uncle Finn said firmly.

Escape

Abby took to humming "Songs of Freedom" while cleaning. This was in between her campaign to get the Veck to use one part of the cave as a toilet instead of the whole place.

"It will get rid of this disgusting smell."

"What is a smell?"

She pointed to the Veck's nose. She pointed to her nose. She sniffed and said "smell?"

If the Veck could shrug he would have shrugged. It really seemed that their sense of smell, vital for hunting, switched off when they came back to the cave.

Did this stop Abby nagging them? Come on, you know Abby better than that by now. It was a long long job but she was up to it. In the end they would have caved in but she intended to escape sooner than that.

The Veck had remarkably strong shoulders and arms. She was not surprised that a gnarl, whatever that was exactly, couldn't fly with their wings. She thought she couldn't manage it either.

She looked out of the front of the cave over the spectacular view of the rolling hills. She wondered if the other clumps of trees she could see were like Gai and if they were all connected with each other. The Veck didn't tell her anything about the mind they shared. She realised that the joint mind wasn't in one place but it was something they all shared with Gai and Ardin. She couldn't imagine Ardin living in such a mess though.

There seemed to be no way out of the cave for anyone who could not fly.

There were eight pairs of wings although there were only four of them in the cave. Far from being able to fly with them, she found she could only just lift them.

Then she had an idea. They were of no use to her and what do you do with rubbish?

The Veck spent most of the day eating or sleeping. It wasn't long to wait until they were all asleep in the darker part of the cave. The wings were stored – well put in an untidy heap – near the entrance where the light was too bright to snooze.

She very carefully dragged one of the wings to the cave mouth trying to make as little noise as possible. They were going to be furious about this but she thought they were under orders from Ardin not to harm her. Well she was about to find out, she thought, as she watched the wing falling through the air. Only seven to go.

She dragged the next wing to the cave-mouth. The wind was getting stronger and and she felt the wing was going to taker her with it to a very unpleasant death in the valley below. She tried to drag two at a time to get the job done before the Veck woke up. Her heart was beating fast and she was sweating despite the fact that the cave mouth was becoming the coldest part of the cave.

One of the Veck woke up as the last two wings were making their way to the bottom of the mountain.

"What on earth are you doing?" He shouted.

"I have thrown the wings out of the cave." This was probably the bravest thing Abby had ever said. The response was surprising.

Anger blazed in the Veck's eyes to begin with. He shouted at Abby and this woke up the other Veck. They looked at Abby. They saw the missing wings. They realised what had happened. They all started making a most extraordinary noise. It was like a cough and a sneeze and a wheeze.

The one who had wakened first put his hand on Abby's shoulder. She thought he was about to throw her out of the cave mouth after the wings. He was very strong. There was nothing she could do to stop him but this was Abby, she would fight tooth and nail.

"I am my father's daughter." She said. She thought it would be her last words.

"That was the funniest thing you have ever done." The Veck's strange noise was laughter. "You are a brave girl. It is pretty bound to be the case that you are your father's daughter by the way. You are stating the obvious. Is it not having a group mind that makes you do that, I wonder?

"You must think we are totally trapped here. You don't realise that we could climb down the mountain but that would be too much like hard work for us and you know we don't do hard work. We will get out the back way. You didn't know about this because we haven't had to use it and the entrance is under a pile of rubbish at the back of the cave. Guess who is going to have to move all the rubbish, Abby?"

It was a pyramid of rubbish in an alcove in the darkest part of the cave. There were twigs and branches. This gave Abby an idea. She found she was getting full of practical ideas these days. She took a straightish branch and bound some twigs to it. After a few attempts she had made a fairly wonky broom.

Fairly wonky it may be, but the Veck were absolutely fascinated by this latest marvel and watched entranced as Abby used it to clear away the mess. She found that she had to go fairly slowly or there was a mess of twigs and she had to reconstruct the broom. To the Veck though it seemed beyond praise.

"If only I could fly on it." Abby joked.

"Pardon?"

"If only I could fly on it like a witch."

"Like a witch?"

"You believe that witches fly on brooms?"

"Well only in fairy stories."

The Veck looked as if they didn't understand.

"It doesn't happen in real life. It only happens in stories. Don't you have stories?"

"Grown ups don't have stories."

Was that a trace of sadness in the Veck? Abby was getting better at reading their feelings now. She could try them with stories some time but she wouldn't because she was going to escape.

The Veck lifted the stone door of the back entrance and said goodbye to Abby as they went off to find their wings. They explained carefully that the door was far too heavy for her to lift so she should just wait for them to get back.

Abby waited. She made herself count to five hundred before she attacked the door. The Veck were not kidding. This was a very heavy door. With her bare hands she would never be able to get out.

Although the door was heavy it had room for hand-holds either side and at the top. The one at the top she realised was bigger than the others. These fine fellows were very strong but there was one thing they didn't know about.

Levers. She had had a lesson about levers. She remembered that a man called Archimedes used to boast "Give me a place to stand and with a lever I will move the whole world." Well her job wasn't nearly as tough as that.

She looked around for the strongest branch she could find. She used it to try to lever the door open. It slipped.

"Hell-fire and damnation" she said. Just as her father would have said. She missed him. She missed Tom and Alfred. Good Lord she even missed Seren. She had to escape before she came over all soppy. That thought made her try again and again

Eventually she shifted the door an inch. She shoved other branches under the sides and had a breather. Lever and wedge. Lever and wedge. In time she had a gap big enough to see a dark staircase leading down into the heart of the mountain.

She had lost weight on her diet of gristle and fat. "I could teach those supermodels a thing or two." she thought as she wriggled through the gap.

A few steps down the staircase and the door fell with a horribly final crash. She was in the dark. She was on a slippery narrow spiral staircase. She could die here. Was she afraid? Well don't be ridiculous she was as scared as Daniel in the Lions den. Actually he wasn't scared. She was as scared as a very scared person.

In the darkness she heard, as if it were real, the voice of her father telling his old bedtime stories about the ancestors. They were an incredibly brave lot in his stories. "They preferred death to slavery, Abby. You are a Cool. We play it cool."

"I am a Cool, I play it cool!" she said out loud as she took another step downwards. Her voice sounded very loud in the darkness. She whispered the next line as she went on her way into the unknown darkness. "I prefer death to slavery."

Conversation with Gai

Gai did not really have conversations with Alfred. It was more like one part of his mind swapping information with another. The gnarl have machines. Gai had never seen the need for machines and knew little of them up until now. Now it was absorbing everything Alfred had got from living with the Professor all those years.

The wheel, the first carts, the steam engine, the train. Gai absorbed this information and opened up a whole new library in its mind to store it all. Then Alfred thought about writing, the invention of the printing press, spelling, then went on to email, the internet and the World Wide Web.

Alfred could feel that Gai was amused by this. Well it is very clumsy. Gai was part of the group mind which spanned the whole earth. The group mind kept knowledge for thousands of years (whatever years were, Alfred patiently explained that too) so no need to write it all down. It was just **there**. As for the world wide web – Alfred had visions of deserts and snowy wastes where creatures very similar to the gnarl lived in great halls of ice. To call them igloos was like calling Buckingham Palace a cottage. The oceans of earth stretching beautiful and blue to the horizon and then below the oceans the great expanse of rock and sand and the vast colourful underwater Gai with fishes swimming in and out of the fronds. Gai really had her own world wide web.

The sight of the fish made Alfred feel hungry. This was very strange because he didn't like eating fish. But Gai did. The fish didn't share the group mind, not until Gai had eaten them anyway.

The gnarl were not part of the group mind. The gnarl who lived above ground in the snowy wastes were but the ones underground were not. They had to **want** to join in and as Alfred could see, they would rather make war. They focussed on weapons and fighting and they were very good at it.

Alfred had a vision of them practising fighting with weapons very like swords and hammers. They had a new weapon too. They were talking about it. They looked forward to using it.

"We must capture a gnarl and find out about this new weapon. First we must raid the weapon hoard closest to here." Alfred thought this but he knew that he was thinking Gai's thoughts now. And he knew that he was going to play a key part in the raid on the weapon hoard.

The following day, Ardin was going to lead a group to attack the weapon hoard. In the tunnels of the gnarl there was no light. Alfred's powers of hearing and his ability to smell out danger would be very valuable to them.

Alfred's mind had a thought all of its own. "I will go with the raiding party. I will willingly face the danger but you must let my people go!"

Gai readily agreed to this. Uncle Finn, Tom and Seren ought to join Gai, they deserved to share in the group mind but if they were not ready they could go back to their ship until they were ready. Abby was another matter. She had been in the hands of the Veck and they shared the group mind and they would have released her, although they liked her cleaning the cave. They couldn't release her because she had escaped. She was nowhere that they could find her.

Abby

Down and down into the darkness. Abby tried reassuring herself out loud but the echoes were frightening. In her own mind she said "I am a Cool. We play it cool. We prefer death to slavery." After a while she decided all the talk of death was getting her down. She tried praying,

"Hail Mary full of grace,

Blessed art thou amongst women

And blessed is the fruit of thy womb, Jesus.

Holy Mary Mother of God

Pray for us sinners, now and at the hour of our death.

Amen"

There was no getting away from death today it seemed. After a while in the darkness her eyes started playing tricks on her. Little circles of light, sometimes blue and sometimes green or yellow started dancing around. She closed her eyes and there the little blighters were again.

"This is the outside of enough. It is bad enough trying to climb down a slippery old spiral staircase without you frolicking around. Are you trying to drive me mad?"

She said this out loud and the word "mad" seemed to echo in the stairwell, or was it inside her head? That really panicked her. Her heart started beating "nineteen to the dozen" as her dad would have said and despite the wretched cold she was sweating.

"I am a Cool. We play it cool." she repeated over and over until her heart started beating normally again.

When she finally saw the flickering yellow light she though that was another trick of her tricky mind. She was on the verge of telling it to "naff off" when she heard the voice.

"Ghash gniggle gerbump" it seemed to say. She stayed stock still but then the light started to go down the stairs and she wanted to follow it. She could hear footsteps and heavy breathing. Whatever else it was, it couldn't possibly be the Veck. She wondered about the gnarl. What were they really like? Was she about to find out?

The light went off into a damp tunnel. She started to follow it but she was suddenly grabbed by small strong hands.

"Gareth Gnarl Gnistle Gnuckalick?"

It seemed to be a question.

"I'm sorry. I don't understand a word of what you are saying."

The gnarl gripped her arms more tightly and repeated the question more loudly. Like an angry British tourist in France he thought that speaking louder would make him understood. It didn't work.

The gnarl looked as if he were about to head-butt her but then another gnarl appeared and apparently ordered him to stop.

Abby was in a quandary. She couldn't speak gnarl. The gnarl couldn't speak English and her remote connection to the shipboard computer was sitting safely in her pack, back in the sacred glade.

The gnarl made a noise which may have been laughter. If so it was a very ugly kind of laughter. It was the laughter of someone who likes being cruel and finds it funny to hurt people. She was dragged along one tunnel after another. In some she had to crawl. Every time she touched the walls she felt they were damp.

She was pushed into a cave and an iron door clanged shut behind her. This cave was very well lit. There were globes which lit it up. The walls were not damp and there was a gnarl looking at her with interest. The main thing she saw was a huge machine which had wrist straps attached to it. She was convinced the gnarl was going to torture her.

The gnarl strapped her wrists to the machine but then to her surprise he then strapped himself to the machine as well.

"Well that's better. Can you understand me now?" He was still speaking the gnarl language but Abby could understand every word.

"You can speak English?"

"I have no idea what English is. This is the machine of understanding. I am the questioner. You will tell me everything. We will start with who you are, why you came into our tunnel and where you come from."

"My name is Abby, Abby Cool. I came into the tunnel because I was escaping from the Veck. I come from a distant planet."

"If you came from a distant planet what were you doing with the Veck?"

"I was a cleaner."

"That is good. We need cleaners, Abby."

"You can't keep me here?"

"Why not?"

She thought quickly. "If you keep me here there will be an earthquake. Your tunnels will collapse and hundreds of you will die."

He called in another gnarl and told him about the earthquake. It never occurred to him to disbelieve Abby because Gai could not lie and the gnarl never had any experience of anyone other than those who shared the group mind.

"There is no way we can fight an earthquake We will have to seek permission to release her."

Abby's heart leapt when she heard that. Getting away was going to be easy. Then her hopes were dashed as the questioner said,

"Yes. After I have finished questioning her of course. Then we can release her to a distant tunnel where an earthquake won't bother us."

The Road to Mandalay

"On the road to Mandalay

Where the flying fishes play,

And the dawn comes up like thunder,

out of China cross the bay." Uncle Finn was always in full voice first thing in the morning. Abby usually threw things at him at this point. Instead he was interrupted in a different way by a different young lady.

"So you have fish that fly?"

Ardin had appeared out of nowhere and was standing in the glade calmly looking at the humans.

"They leap out of the water and it looks as if they are flying. They don't have wings so they don't fly long distances." Tom knew everything and could never resist showing it.

Ardin was solid blue and her tail was neatly curled around her waist. She noticed the humans looking at her and said proudly,

"This is what you call combat readiness. We don't have names but we are given colours. I will stay this colour until the battle is won or I am dead. As for the tail, it is not really a weapon so it is kept out of the way. I have not brought any weapons with me because..." she held out her hand to Tom, "I come in peace."

"Where is Abby?"

"Alas I can only tell you that she is alive and well and we will return her to you as soon as possible."

"You don't know where she is? Wasn't she kidnapped on your orders?"

"Yes but then she escaped. She is a very resourceful girl. She is her father's daughter as she put it. Finn, you can be proud of her. We will return her to you or perish in the attempt."

"You talk a lot about dying."

"It is how we prepare for battle. We think of ourselves as dead. We think of our souls going on to a better place. We make our peace with death."

"We are running out of food here."

"Yes we have been monitoring your discussions."

"Eavesdropping, you mean." Seren said angrily.

"We have dropped no eaves. It is a ridiculous expression. I don't care if you call it earwigging, being a Nosy Parker or dropping the eaves. This is our sacred grove and no stranger is to leave it alive. You are breaking that rule. It is a rule which has existed since the dawn of time. All strangers who have ever come here have become part of Gai.

"You are to be released back to your ship if you insist that you will not become one with Gai. We will wait until you are ready. Your leader has more sense than you have. He has become one with Gai."

"Alfred. Are you telling us he is dead?"

"I didn't say dead. He is very much alive. He is more alive than he has ever been in his life now that he has become one with Gai. He is going into battle with us though and he has had to prepare himself for death as we do. He made one condition for going into battle with us though. He said "Let my people go!" in fact he sang it which was very strange.

"Alfred has given his life for us." Tom was appalled.

"Not necessarily," Uncle Finn was quick to see the bright side. "What are the chances in this battle?"

Then Ardin explained all about the gnarl and their anti-social behaviour. She explained exactly what Alfred was to do in the raid. She could not lie but she did not mention the strong suspicion that Abby was in the hands of the gnarl. It was not a fact after all.

Then she pointed to Gai, where a long path had opened up as she was speaking so that the trio could return to the ship.

Finn was the last to leave. He spoke quietly to Ardin. "We must go back to the ship. There is something I left there but let me tell you this, Ardin. I'll be back."

Alfred the warrior

Alfred was born a warrior. All French Bulldogs are. Faced with a larger dog or faced with something unknown – whether it is an alien or a traffic cone – they go into a fighting stance and utter the most unearthly sound on this or any other planet. They always run towards danger, not away from it. It is a wonder that any of them get beyond puppy-hood.

However, he had never come across anything like this before. Ardin and her followers were kneeling in the sacred glade. (Alfred was not a one for kneeling so he sat down – they didn't mind) They were all the colours of the rainbow and there was a heap of horrible-looking blades and hammers of gnarl manufacture ready for them to take up. They were talking about death. To be exact Ardin was broadcasting her thoughts about death, thoughts which came directly from Gai.

"Death does not cut short your life. Death infinitely extends your life. We who have been part of Gai on Earth become part of a greater Gai that spans the universe. Our minds are freed of these bodies. Our bodies return to Gai. It is not death that is to be feared.

"It is killing which is to be feared. The gnarl will all fight. The males, the females, even the little gnarlings. As we hate weapons and violence they love it. With our pitiful stock of stolen weapons they will destroy many of us. That is why we are taking this weapon hoard. It could save lives in the long run. Whatever happens there is to be no killing of gnarlings. They are to be disarmed. It is better to die than to kill a gnarling. One day they will grow up. One day they will join Gai.

"We have been building tunnels in secret. The gnarl have found some of these tunnels and of course they have destroyed them but there are three still intact. Two other groups are attacking through the other tunnels. There is just a wall of earth between our tunnel and the tunnels of the gnarl."

"Grey." she finished.

A girl stepped forward. She was so similar to Ardin it was hard to tell which was which but she was in fact entirely grey. She distributed the horrible weapons. The others took them reluctantly. There were not enough for everyone. Grey spoke to the ones without weapons.

"Yours is the place of honour. You will come last and you will take the weapons of the fallen to continue the fight."

They accepted this without a question. Their thoughts were focussed on death.

Alfred thought his place was the place of honour. He was going first. His eyes were no better than theirs. His ears and his nose were going to lead them in the darkness of the gnarl tunnel.

The company made their way to the tunnel entrance. They were silent. Even their thoughts seemed to be quiet. Alfred was trying to shake off all this talk about death and think positively. French Bulldogs all think they are immortal. He was not ready to join the universal mind. Not today, thank you.

The tunnel was well lit and quite high enough for them to walk upright with Alfred proudly leading them. They put out all of the lights as they prepared to smash through the remaining mud between them and the tunnel of the gnarl.

There were no watches to synchronise. Their minds were in tune with the other raiding parties. They smashed through at the same instant.

Alfred was in the tunnels of the gnarl. He smelt gnarl for the first time. He could hear gnarl in the distance and thanks to Gai he could understand what they were saying. The tunnel was slowly filling up with Ardin's company. They were as silent as they could be but to Alfred they were making an appalling noise.

"Did you hear something?" The voice of the gnarl was very distant. It actually said "ghar glisty google?" but since Alfred could translate it is all in English from here on in.

"Yes. Go and call out the guard and tell them to keep quiet. Whatever it is we will take it by surprise. See if you can get permission to use the secret weapon."

"It's funny."

"Funny" the first voice was outraged that anything should be funny.

"Well it is funny. If it is slaves of Gai then they have come seeking death. The secret weapon will be the answer to all their wishes."

Despite himself the first gnarl gave a chuckle which was quickly suppressed. There was no joy in his laughter.

Battle underground

Alfred ran unerringly towards the foe. The tunnels twisted and turned, they branched into a hundred side tunnels but the smell of gnarl was unmistakeable and Alfred could always find the right one. The company were hard on his heels but he was always in the lead.

Suddenly he came upon the gnarl. There was a faint light coming round the edges of an iron door. Suddenly the door burst open and a squad of heavily-armed gnarl came into the corridor.

This was a challenge. Alfred responded as he always did. The weird unearthly noise he let out echoed horribly in the tunnel and the gnarl were terrified. They had never heard anything like it and they had never seen anything like Alfred. In fact there was not a single dog on this Earth.

Taking advantage of their confusion, Ardin pushed them back into the cave beyond the iron door and the company fought the gnarl in the sudden light. The light was glinting off a thousand weapons. Alfred had led them straight to the weapon hoard.

"Dog eat dog" is a very unfair expression. Dogs very rarely eat dogs. And because they do not eat them they very seldom kill them. Alfred had his first taste of watching creatures kill each other and as Ardin had predicted it was a taste that made him sick.

There was a room off the weapon cave and as the battle was at its most fierce a group of gnarl burst through the door. Four gnarl armed with vicious blades came through the door but they were protecting two gnarl carrying the secret weapon.

It was a kind of gun which is called on our Earth a "blunderbuss". One gnarl was lighting a taper at one end of the blunderbuss and the other was aiming it at the company. The gnarl who had been fighting them dropped to the floor.

There was a horrible pause as the company looked down the enormous barrel of the blunderbuss and wondered what on earth was going to happen.

"Get down!" was Alfred's thought and he thought it so fiercely that it was like a shouted order. Many of the company threw themselves to the ground. They survived.

The ones who had been too slow were cut down with nails and shards of metal as the horrific blast of the blunderbuss deafened everyone in the cave. The air was filled with a foul stinking smoke.

Alfred didn't hold back now. He threw himself at the gnarl who were holding the blunderbuss. The barrel was red hot and they knew it wouldn't fire again. The gnarl dropped it and fled back behind the iron door.

Ardin was one of those who had obeyed Alfred. There was a horrible ringing in her ears and the smell was, if anything getting worse.

She stood by the bodies of her fallen comrades and looked gravely at Alfred. "They had their secret weapon. We had ours. Without Alfred we would all be lying dead right now."

She became businesslike. "We are not out of this yet. We will have to fight a rearguard action to get these weapons out of here. Albert and I will take pride of place at the back. If we have to we will die fighting the gnarl patrols if they attack. The noise must have brought some of them running.

"What do you call this weapon, Alfred? It is clear that you know what it is."

"It is a blunderbuss, a kind of gun. It is a very crude one. There is gunpowder in that end and anything at all, shot, nails, anything metal in the other."

"Well we will take it with us. Can you make gunpowder?"

"I know what goes into it. It is sulphur, carbon and saltpeter. The Professor used to make fireworks with it. It will take time though and it all depends when the gnarl are ready for all-out war."

"Well taking the weapon hoard has perhaps bought us some time," said Ardin.

The other companies finally arrived from the other tunnels. There was nothing left for them but lifting and carrying. They had missed their chance to die. Some were disappointed. Ardin picked the most disappointed ones to join her in the rearguard. It was a long long trek through the tunnels. Alfred's skills of navigation were no longer needed. Gai was guiding them back.

Alfred, Ardin and three friends Ardin called Red, Green and Black took up the rear ready to turn and fight the minute they detected any gnarl coming towards them.

The gnarl did not attack. What were they waiting for?

Suddenly, Black noticed something, "We are being followed but not by a patrol. There is only one set of footsteps." Black had not had her ears blasted by the blunderbuss noise.

Alfred, however, recognised the smell. He would have smiled if his face were not a permanent smile like all French Bulldogs. "It's Uncle Finn!" He sent out the thought.

"Is that Uncle Finn?" Ardin whispered urgently.

"I ain't your blooming uncle!" came back the unmistakeable voice. "Still Ardin. I told you I'd be back didn't I."

"It's dangerous in here."

"So I understand. That is why you guys need my help. It comes at no charge." Uncle Finn said as he joined them. Alfred sought him in the dark and Uncle Finn started fussing over him.

"I've brought you..."

"Shhh" interrupted Black. "Gnarl. Coming this way."

Secret weapons

There were only a handful of gnarl as far as Black's ears could tell. Perhaps they had another blunderbuss.

Their fears were confirmed when they saw the glowing taper being brought to the gunpowder.

They dived for the floor.

"They have a gun." Ardin explained unnecessarily.

"That's not a gun. This is a gun." Finn said.

Finn had picked up a surprisingly powerful pistol from a bloke he met in an East End pub who traded it for a consignment of merchandise Finn was anxious to get rid of.

He had no skill with a weapon. He had something much better. Luck.

Three shots rang out. Three gnarl fell dead. The blunderbuss fired harmlessly into the wall of the tunnel.

Uncle Finn picked up the blunderbuss and handed it to Ardin.

"Look, you guys get out. I will deal with any gnarl who follow you. I have unfinished business."

The rearguard consulted briefly. Alfred said he would stay to keep an eye on Uncle Finn and that was good enough for them.

"You mean an ear and a nose of course." Ardin couldn't resist stroking Alfred's ears before she took her leave.

"Good boy, Alfred. This is going to be dangerous," said Uncle Finn quietly.

"I know perfectly well that it is going to be dangerous. I won't let you die. At the very least I won't let you die alone." Alfred thought. He expressed this by nuzzling Uncle Finn's leg and Uncle Finn understood.

Uncle Finn had not thought about death for hours beforehand and he did not have a problem killing the kidnappers who were holding his daughter. He made this clear to the first pair of gnarl they met. They were carrying torches and they could see Alfred and were afraid.

He pointed the gun at them. They had no idea what the gun was so they kept coming. He shot one and raced forward to catch the other. The one he shot was not dead and its cries were terrible as its black blood spilled in the corridor.

He did not speak gnarl. He did not need to. He disarmed the startled gnarl and looked him straight in the eye. He said the one word, "Abby." The gnarl did not seem to know what he was talking about.

He tried questions like "Where is Abby?" but the repetition of the name did not seem to help. He held the gun to the gnarl's head. The gnarl spat at him.

He couldn't shoot an unarmed enemy. The Cools don't do that. It just isn't cool. He pushed the gnarl away. Immediately, Alfred set on him, jumping up and growling. The terrified gnarl fled with Alfred in pursuit. Yapping at his heels.

The gnarl led them straight into a dining room where about fifteen gnarl were having a meal. The smell of the food made Uncle Finn hungry. He fired the gun once at the ceiling to get their undivided attention. He grabbed the nearest gnarl and pointed the gun to her head. "Abby?"

"Abby?" he said again louder. One of the gnarl stood up and put up his hands in the universal gesture of surrender showing that he was unarmed.

"No tricks now!" Uncle Finn said sternly. The gnarl could not understand any of the words but recognised the tone. He answered with a stream of gnarlish talk which Alfred interpreted as "Don't shoot me. I am taking you there as fast as I can. I have gnarlings of my own."

Alfred tried in vain to convey this information to Uncle Finn but he had other things on his mind. Abby was being held in a small cave with an iron door. The jailer refused to give up the keys and attacked Uncle Finn. He got a bullet in the mouth for his trouble and Uncle Finn got the keys.

They could hear Abby behind the door shouting, "What is all the ruddy noise? I am trying to sleep in here!"

Uncle Finn was too pleased to hear her voice to say anything but Alfred, who seldom barked, thought this was an occasion to do so.

"Alfred? Good Heavens. It's Alfred. Have they captured you too, lovely dog. How dare they? How dare they?"

Uncle Finn opened the door of the cell and Abby flew out and right into his arms. Her clothes were dirty and torn and she looked terribly thin and drawn after her ordeal.

For a long time Uncle Finn just held the ex-prisoner while his prisoner, the gnarl, sneaked quietly away to raise the alarm.

"Now all we have to do is get out of here. I am sorry to say I have no idea of the way so what we will do is.."

"I do." said Abby cutting across Uncle Finn's flow of talk. He looked at her in surprise.

She pointed to an adjacent door.

"The questioner interrogated me for hours and hours and hours in that room. This tunnel leads to another tunnel. There are two. We need the one that slopes upwards. It is as dark as the pits of Hell so we could do with one of your torches. You remember the really cheap ones that work half the time."

"The upward sloping tunnel leads to a gigantic stiral sparecase.. a squiral stareplace...one of those ones that go up and round."

Uncle Finn looked at Alfred who was not at his best on staircases.

"I will carry you Alfred. Just don't do what you did last time I carried you!"

Alfred thought Uncle Finn had forgotten all about the time he had weed all over his jacket when he was a puppy and thought this was hardly the time to bring it up.

"Let's go." They ran down the tunnel.

The torch was just as Abby had said. Uncle Finn had to keep banging it to get it to work. Eventually they worked out that it would work best pointing to the ceiling. Then the battery started to fade.

Abby kept up a non-stop tale of woe about how the Veck had treated her and made suggestions about what Uncle Finn could do with the gun when they got to the cave. If and when they got to the cave that is.

They reached the staircase without any gnarl approaching them.

Alfred could hear the patter of tiny feet behind them. It sounded as if one gnarling had followed them from the dining cave but the footsteps stopped when they stopped. The gnarling was in no hurry to join them it seemed.

Flight of the Veck

The torches gave up the ghost half way up the long staircase. Alfred was unfazed by this and of course Finn Cool was frightened of nothing. He was doubly so (if that is possible) with his daughter back again. So Abby, who had been down this staircase before, had no choice but to be brave and not to think even for a moment about the long drop if she missed her footing on the slippery worn stairs.

In the end there came a point at which they could go no further. They pushed at the door but, brave as he was, Uncle Finn did not have the strength of the exceptional arm muscles of the Veck.

Arthur sent an urgent thought to Gai and the Veck were alerted to their presence. One of them single-handedly lifted the heavy stone door and held it above his head like a big show-off.

Uncle Finn came out of the doorway and immediately pointed his gun at the nearest Veck. He pulled the trigger just as Alfred took a flying leap at his arm and deflected his aim so the bullet went harmlessly into the cave wall.

"What are you playing at Alfred. You are supposed to be on our side."

"Well we are on your side." said the Veck.

"Well I don't think so. You forget that you enslaved my daughter."

"Well the reason for that was that she attacked Ardin. An attack on one of us is an attack on all of us. If you shared the group mind you would understand that. As you don't you are little better than the gnarl.

"Anyway, Abby's debt is paid in full and we want to return her to her family. Abby, Alfred, who is this stranger and what is that weapon in his hand?"

"Well I told you I was my father's daughter. This is my father. You might have worked that out from him saying you enslaved his daughter!" Abby said. "And I am still waiting for my cleaner's wages from you cheapskates."

"I have told you before, Abby. We do not have money, so there will be no wages. A free flight back to your ship for all of you is what we offer. Take it or leave it."

"We will take it. Look, I am sorry I tried to kill you, earlier." said Uncle Finn, "shall we let bygones be bygones?"

"If you people had any elementary logic you would know that bygones are bygones whether we let them or not. I am interested in that weapon of yours though. With a few of those the gnarl would be what you might call child's play to deal with."

"There is only one but I think Ardin may be planning to make some imitations of the gnarl' weapon. A blunderbuss would be easier to make."

"But it would involve those dreaded words 'hard work' boys. I can't see you being keen on that."

"We do not work." The Veck said in unison.

"You know, I was a student once myself." said Uncle Finn. "I graduated from the school of hard knocks to the university of life. And in all that time I never lived in such squalor as you lads do. You know I could do you a deal on a very nice little vacuum cleaner. It's a labour-saving device. A device to take the drudgery out of keeping a filthy cave slightly less filthy and I can get you a very special price...

"Now I know what you're going to say. You don't have money but you lads can **fly.** I mean to say, that means we can work out some kind of deal."

"Well we will discuss that later." said one of the Veck.

"And the question of exactly how you are going to get a hoover ten light years through space." thought Alfred. The Veck caught his thought and they marvelled at it.

"Finn Cool." said one of the Veck in awe, "You can tell stories. You are your daughter's father indeed. Alfred tells us that she told the gnarl that there would be an earthquake if they didn't release her and they had to believe her because the group mind cannot lie. They didn't know that she was like you. That is amazing. That really is a secret weapon."

While they had been talking, Alfred felt and smelt a little gnarling creeping up on him. He was about to get ready to attack when he felt the little gnarling's hand stroking his ears. It didn't find Alfred frightening as the older gnarl did. The gnarling was young enough to be open to new creatures in his life.

Alfred was quite ready to have the little chap stroke him but the Veck were appalled.

"Close the back door. We don't want any more of them up here. Alfred move away from that thing so we can deal with it properly."

Alfred knew that "deal with it properly" meant throwing it out of the cave-mouth.

Alfred's thoughts blazed up so that all the Veck had to pay attention. "It is not an it, it is a "he". He is coming with us and that is not negotiable."

The gnarling

"Gnarl must be killed. Or enslaved obviously. This one is too puny for a slave."

"Even if gnarl must be killed. Gnarlings must not. They can be changed, tamed, convinced. They can be made less violent. Although the Veck..." Alfred left that thought unfinished. Membership of the joint mind hadn't knocked off all the rough edges of the Veck as yet.

Abby put her arm around the gnarling. Unlike the adults, the gnarlings are covered in a browny green fur and the gnarling responds to stroking by making a noise similar to purring.

The Veck saw they were not going to have a chance to kill this one; well, not yet anyway.

The Veck and Uncle Finn with a few comments from Abby had a long discussion about this. Meanwhile the gnarling and Alfred went off in search of scraps. Abby did not want to watch them eating fat and gristle and she went to join the others in a huddle.

She saw that the Veck respected her father. He had never seen anything like their strength but they had never come across anything like his mind.

Alfred knew well that although he could eat anything, and often did, he would be sick later. The thought of being sick in flight was unpleasant but Uncle Finn had not actually told him not to eat the scraps.

Alfred and the gnarling had eaten together. As Alfred thought this made them "companions" - well that meant people who shared bread but he didn't eat bread.

Finn insisted on coming back to Alfred and the gnarling after the decision had been taken. He had his jumper in his hand.

"You are coming with us, young Luke but..."and he put his jumper over his head like a hood, "if you will not be turned to the good side of the force, then you will meet your destiny."

Abby was creased up with laughter although the gnarling did not understand a word, he had a try at laughing. From that day on all the family called him 'Luke'. gnarl do not name their children. In fact nobody on earth seemed to have a name for life.

"Hang on, dad. Isn't your destiny just a word for 'what happens to you'? So he is bound to meet his destiny whatever he does."

"All right Miss Smarty-pants. We had best be out of here or you will be as literal as your Veck friends. You and I are going first. Then Alfred is coming with young Luke here."

"I thought her name was Abby Cool not Smarty-pants. You humans insist on having names and then make up new ones. We only tell the truth and Abby we give you our word that Alfred and Luke will arrive safe and well. They are lighter than you anyway.

"We want to thank you for the cleaning and we give you a present."

The Veck had mended her broom and gave it to her

"Now we must go unless you want to fly back like a witch."

The flight by daylight was amazing. There were great rolling hills of white like snow and rivers and lakes of the deepest blue. The hills were golden and the various Gai they passed were a blur of glorious colour.

Abby had the wind blowing in her hair and almost parting her from her precious witches' broom. And despite the height she didn't feel afraid for a minute. The Veck were strong, she couldn't really tell but she thought it was the very Veck who had kidnapped her. And they always told the truth. If they weren't such a shower of lazy slobs she would have liked them.

Uncle Finn still had his remote so he was able to open the door of the ship. Tom and Seren rushed to the noise and were startled to see Abby, Uncle Finn and two Veck standing there. Tom rushed to attack the Veck who was holding Abby. Abby struck him with the handle of the broomstick.

"Ow. What on earth is going on?"

"These Veck have just brought us safely through the air from their cave. The least they deserve is a cup of tea.

"Tea?"

"Well how about a glass of water? You must accept our hospitality you know." Uncle Finn said, and then to Tom. Get a couple of mats will you and put them down outside the door."

When the mats were brought he addressed the Veck. "You wipe your feet on the mat before coming in. It is a custom."

"Is this another of your stories, Finbar Cool?"

"Just do it, lads."

The Veck went through the unfamiliar action of wiping their feet. One tried to pick up the mat to do it. Tom put him right.

They sat in the ship and Uncle Finn made a great song and dance of telling the story of how Abby had been rescued and Alfred was the hero of the hour. Abby went up to Seren and asked her quietly to come with her to her sleeping area. Abby pulled up her mattress and sure enough there was Seren's missing red top.

"I took it because I was being a bitch. I am sorry."

"You can keep it." said Seren. She meant, "I don't want it now you have had your thieving hands on it."

"I don't want to take it until you really want me to have it Seren. I will wash it for you."

"You've changed." said Seren with a bit of sarcasm in her voice.

"I hope I have." said Abby.

This made Seren pause. Then she said, "How stupid we both are!" and threw her arms around a startled Abby. "Thank God you are safe. Welcome back Abby. Welcome back."

When they went back to the table it was on the tip of Tom's tongue to ask "What have you two been crying about" but in his heart he knew better. He went and hugged Abby and there were no tears in his eyes. Definitely none. Maybe one in just one eye.

The flight of the Veck

Alfred had never flown before. No dog on earth had ever flown like this. The strong shoulders of the Veck controlled the wings while his hands held Alfred as firmly as if they were taking a walk in the park. Alfred felt safe and comfortable despite the great height and speed because the Veck was comfortable here.

Alfred was not only colour-blind but he was also short-sighted. The Veck was not. Alfred could look through the Veck's eyes and a whole amazing world of colour burst into his mind.

The clouds, the sky, the rivers and the fields, the grey gazelle-like creatures he saw in flocks on the plain were just amazing. The animals he saw made him want to swoop down and hunt them. He realised the Veck's ideas were leaking into his mind too.

And as they rushed through the air, he had a mental conversation with the Veck as calmly as if they were in a drawing-room.

"Your mission if you want it."the Veck began

"I already accepted it by joining Gai and now you in the group mind."

"I know I was just being polite. Your mission will be to turn the gnarling."

"Luke." put in Alfred.

"Ridiculous name, yes 'Luke' if you must. Your mission will be to turn Luke, Finn Cool, Seren, Tom and Abby to the group mind. The priority will be the gnarlin...Luke. We will have to prepare for war. The group mind hates war. And the Veck have become part of the group mind. We hate war too."

"You are OK with killing though."

"We are hunters. You have to make allowances."

"You do realise that you won't be able to hunt gnarl if they join the group mind."

"We will worry about that if and when it happens. Alfred. Is this what you call 'teasing'."

Alfred laughed inwardly and the Veck understood.

Luke was terrified. There was no calming conversation and no meeting of minds for him. Towards the end of the flight however, he was thrilled rather than frightened. He had realised that the Veck was not going to drop him because it would have done so by now. As they were skimming the treetops on the way to the ship he was a bit sad that the flight was ending.

"If you say 'What the Hell's that?' again I will stick your head down the toilet." Seren reprimanded Tom. "Now come and stroke Luke. You know full well you want to."

Seren and Abby were sitting either side of Luke and trying to make him comfortable. They were both discussing how to adapt some of Tom's clothes for him and Tom was not best pleased about this idea.

"The gnarl are meat-eaters, you know." said Tom who knew everything and was certainly not going to stroke Luke while anyone could see him do so. "How do you think about that Abby."

"Teasing vegetarians is the lowest form of wit." Abby responded. "I love Alfred and he loves meat. I have learned to live and let live. So should you."

Tom went off to do something important. He wouldn't tell the girls what it was because he didn't know himself. He wandered into the ship where the Veck were sitting and chatting with Uncle Finn.

Uncle Finn had a bottle of something the prof definitely did not know was aboard the ship. It was the Prof's twelve-year-old single malt whisky and he was sharing it generously with the two Veck. They decided that Finn was their best mate in the world after the first glass.

The Veck were eager, to be exact, through them the group mind was eager, to learn about stories from Finn. They had stories – the tales of those who had died in battle or died rescuing fallen heroes or just plain died. They were all true stories.

"All good stories begin, 'Once upon a time..." said Uncle Finn. Those words drew Tom like a magnet and he drew up a chair to share the table with them. He tried to share the whisky too but Uncle Finn was too quick for him. He had to make do with lemonade.

"Once upon a time there were three bears..." He told the story with his own little changes.

For example he insisted that the youngest bear had lost a lot of fur so he was called 'Fred Bear'. Tom had laughed his socks off about this when he was a toddler.

Now he just felt he had to tell the Veck that bears were animals who did not live in houses or eat porridge. They dismissed this impatiently and turned to Uncle Finn.

"So we know that the story is not true."

Finn nodded.

"So where is the truth?"

"It is like this." Finn was unusually thoughtful. "If you go to those two girls outside and mention any part of that story they immediately know what you are talking about. Even the Prof who built this ship used to talk about the 'Goldilocks zone". The story becomes a part of the way we think. And that is the truth."

Tom had never seen Uncle Finn serious for such a long period of time and he insisted on him telling some of his jokes right away. The Veck sat in silence during Uncle Finn's jokes, even the one about his aunt and the raspberry which as ever had Tom rolling about on the floor laughing.

As this was going on the group mind was opening two whole new virtual libraries for fairy tales and jokes. These libraries did not have books or even CDs. It was a group mind and it was everywhere.

For days Alfred had to dictate stories into these libraries. He could do it while eating, walking or sleeping so the others didn't notice him doing it. He needed a good long walk every day and it was usually Tom who volunteered to do it.

Alfred had to explain the difference between lies and stories. The group mind eventually decided there were stories, there were lies and there was something in-between. This was labelled "lories" in the end.

Abby and Seren were spending their time and love on Luke. They taught him to speak English with a lot of nursery rhymes and stories, endless stories. Gnarlings are never given that kind of attention and love. It explains a lot about why the gnarl are the way they are.

Alfred didn't mind. Or at least he told himself he shouldn't mind and he tried not to. After all he was thinking of a way the coming war could be avoided. Luke was central to his plan.

For all the while they were carrying on with their lives, the gnarl were preparing for war. The taking of their weapon hoard levelled the odds a little bit but the gnarl were hard-working and they produced weapons rather than anything else so they would be ready to go to war in the near future.

Uncle Finn had become a drinking buddy for the Veck. Before hunting (they always hunted at night) they would come and chat with him. They soon finished off the Prof's whisky but they had a drink of their own. In true Veck fashion they had never thought of a name for it. After one glass, Uncle Finn decided "firewater" would do nicely and they were happy to go along with that.

One night they discussed the coming battle. The Veck repeated the idea that you prepare for battle by preparing to die. There had not been a war with the gnarl for a very long time. Certainly before the fathers of this generation of Veck were born. The group mind had vivid memories of these wars.

The gnarl would fight ruthlessly. Anyone they conquered would be enslaved. The gnarl did not care whether their slaves lived or died. Uncle Finn was about to comment that the Veck seemed to be the same way but he thought better of it. It had taken some time to defeat the gnarl but although they were excellent warriors they were very inefficient slave-drivers and easy to escape from. They never counted their slaves for example. Uncle Finn tucked this piece of knowledge away for future use.

Ardin and her people were working hard to reproduce the blunderbuss and Alfred's knowledge of gunpowder gave them hope they could defend themselves. The gnarl were also working hard. They would have more weapons than their enemies. The war would be delayed until they reached that state.

The humans talked together about this, quite forgetting that Alfred would pass on anything to the group mind.

"Uncle Finn, are you going to be a gun for hire for Gai?"

Uncle Finn looked as if he liked the idea of that but he loved a tease.

"Why not a gun for hire for the gnarl."

The children were outraged. Uncle Finn laughed. "Of course I will fight for Gai. If it ever comes to that." He added mysteriously.

The Gnarling goes home

Uncle Finn gave names to the two Veck who were always coming round to share firewater and a yarn with him. He called one Andrew and the other Bernard. He reserved Claude for the one who always stayed home to guard the cave. This was rather spoilt because after an evening of jawing and firewater he would often say a cheery 'Goodnight Andrew' to Bernard and vice versa.

"Why must you name things and people? We never bother and we manage." said Bernard (or possibly Andrew)

"Well take young Luke, the gnarling. He will never have a name back home from what you tell me. He isn't an individual with a soul and more practically the gnarl probably don't know he's missing. gnarl do not have "parents" after they are weaned. They either survive in the tunnels or they don't. It is supposed to make them tough. They certainly are tough.

"We have souls! I have a soul. 'Bernard' if I must call him that, he has a soul. We do not have names because I am not better than he is and he is not better than I am. We are Veck plural. We are Veck singular. "

Uncle Finn thought about this while Bernard tried out a joke on him. They struggled to understand Uncle Finn's jokes but they were determined to have their own jokes.

"What is the difference between a gnarl and a pile of poo?"

"I don't know what is the difference between a gnarl and a pile of poo?" Uncle Finn had heard something a bit like this before somewhere.

"That's funny I don't know either" said the Veck. The pair of Veck fell about laughing at that one. Uncle Finn laughed along.

The Veck he had been calling Bernard looked seriously at him. "Finn Cool, you laugh although you do not find it funny."

"Yes. It is a laugh of companionship. Now let's have a little drink of companionship to celebrate."

When Finn had refilled the glasses he asked, "Can a child join the joint mind? I mean a child as young as Abby for example."

"Abby is not a child." The Veck was adamant about that. "Abby may have been a child when she came to us. She is no child now."

Uncle Finn decided to take that as a compliment.

Andrew, who had had less to drink than Bernard, solemnly turned to Tom and said, "Nobody here is too young to join the group mind, you just have to have the sense to do so. Age is no barrier. "

Tom usually tagged along drinking lemonade and listening to the talk. He smiled at the fact they considered him an adult.

"You include Luke?" Tom asked.

"Luke, the gnarling, of course. Albert thinks he is ready. Albert can see into minds far more than anyone else. We trust his judgement."

"Is it safe for him to go back when he has joined the group mind; won't the gnarl kill him?"

"gnarl never kills gnarl." was the surprising answer. "Veck never kill Veck. Gai does not kill at all. Even animals do not kill their own kind."

Joining the group mind was very simple. Luke put his hand on Alfred's head as he had done a thousand times before. Every time he did it, he felt the need deep inside himself to join with the group mind. There was no ceremony. There was nothing to sign. He became one with the group mind.

He sat down on the floor. He was overwhelmed.

"Strong is that one with the force!" Uncle Finn wanted to lighten the mood.

"Not the police force eh?" Luke had heard a lot of Uncle Finn's stories by now.

"Wash your mouth out. Nobody mentions the rozzers in this house." Finn was pretending to be most offended.

"Ship." corrected Tom, who knew everything.

It was an anxious time. They knew Luke had to go back to the tunnels of the gnarl. They believed that he would be safe but there were no guarantees.

"What if the gnarl can detect the group mind in Luke?" asked Abby. She really was very fond of Luke. Apart from Alfred, Tom was a bit jealous of that too.

Nobody had an answer to that. They looked at Alfred and he shook his head in an almost human gesture.

"Everything could depend on Luke you know."

"Well that's why I called him Luke isn't it?" Uncle Finn for once was unsure of what to do. The gnarl were hastening towards war. He was cleaning his gun and searching around for ammunition that would fit it. His back pack was an Aladdin's Cave of things including ammunition for a surprising variety of weapons. He held on to them 'just in case' but would not tell anyone 'in case of what'.

He had an idea of lighting a fire and leaving the ammunition in the fire in hopes of killing gnarl. The possibility of killing practically anyone who came near the fire probably meant this was impractical except..well he thought there might be an exception.

There was a raiding party the following night. He had volunteered to take part. The idea was to stop the gnarl making blunderbusses. Gai had a good idea of a location and new tunnels had been dug in secret. It was just a matter of time before the gnarl found the tunnels but it was hoped that they would not find them so soon.

Alfred opted to go along with Finn rather than with Ardin's group. The idea of thinking about death all the way there didn't particularly appeal to him at the moment. Even Uncle Finn's jokes were better than that. Well, he felt a loyalty to Uncle Finn so he would tolerate the jokes.

Luke knew all about this of course. He had spent days exploring the stories and jokes in the group mind. Alfred had added thousands by this time. He knew all about the attack and he intended to tag along. Uncle Finn just thought he was incredibly brave and told him so, at least twelve times until Tom, Abby and Seren made a pact.

"What is a pact exactly?" Abby asked innocently.

"Well you could call it an agreement. It is a binding agreement." said Tom

"You mean you're going to tie us up?" said Seren.

"Far from it. We are going to take these knives."

Tom pulled back the blanket on his bunk and there were the most horrible-looking knives in Uncle Finn's collection.

"Then what?" Seren asked.

"We wait until they set off to the raid. We wait about a minute. Then we set off after them. They may need our help."

"A minute? We haven't got a watch between us now. You remember we traded them with the Veck for firewater and they gave us some watered down rubbish. We had to throw it away in the end." Seren sometimes wondered why she went along with her brother's ideas so often. He wondered the same thing.

"Well we count 'one little second two little second three little seconds'..." Tom explained.

"Oh don't tell me, let me guess. Can it be 'four little seconds'." said Abby. They all laughed at that.

Seren added, "Surely you could just count your heartbeats to work out the time."

"No." Tom was firm about this, "Your heartbeat varies. If you are excited or scared (not that any of us are scared) then your heartbeat would be faster."

So they agreed with Tom. It was usually the quickest way to end an argument.

When the night of the raid came everyone was scared, or excited perhaps, even Uncle Finn who counted his bullets and checked his gun more times than he could remember.

There was a strange smell in the tunnel. It smelt like a really cheap aftershave. Eventually Uncle Finn owned up to being the one wearing it.

"Well I figured I probably wasn't ever going to sell it."

"Shhh" said Ardin. "We are nearly thcro."

They came to a wall of earth. As the company halted, Alfred could hear footsteps, three people were following them. He didn't alert anybody. He recognised the smell of Tom,

Seren and Abby straight away. He was concerned that they were here but hoped he could keep them out of trouble. It was his job to defend them or die in the attempt. That stuff about dying again. He was getting tired of it.

As soon as they were a few yards inside the tunnel they realised they had made a serious mistake. gnarl were coming at them from both directions. Ardin made a decision on the spot. They would make towards the place the blunderbusses were being made.

"Place of honour." was all she said to Finn and Alfred. Finn checked the safety catch on his gun and remembered that it didn't have one. You get what you pay for.

He could hear the gnarl himself now, or so he thought. He raised his gun to fire. Alfred bit his knee.

"Blimey Alfred. What is it?"

Finn's mind was in such an excited state that Alfred's thought got right through to him, "Tom, Seren and Abby."

The darkness was complete when the three arrived. Finn's relief that he hadn't killed them was replaced with a conviction that the gnarl patrol bearing down on them was about to do the job for him.

If the gnarl patrol had been carrying a blunderbuss then this story would have a very different ending. The gnarl had found out the hard way that if a large patrol had a blunderbuss it was a bad idea. The chances were that several of them would lose arms and legs, not to mention lives, in a friendly fire incident. The blunderbuss was a most unsafe weapon and often went off unexpectedly .

When Alfred judged they were close enough he sent the thought "FIRE!" to Uncle Finn and Uncle Finn pulled the trigger. He held it down while the gun fired three times. In the confined space it was likely several gnarl would be killed or injured. The rest did not hang about to find out.

They ran away. Uncle Finn wanted to get the three children - "Two children and one adult" as Abby had been saying too often lately – to safety.

"You've proved how brave you are coming down here. Now Alfred and I are the rearguard and we order you to leave the tunnel as soon as we get back to the exit. Do you understand?" Finn said. He waited.

Tom acted as spokesman, "Yes we understand."

As they ran down the tunnel Tom suddenly said, "The gnarl are regrouping. They are coming back towards us. There is a tunnel off to the left. We should hide in there. " It took Finn a moment to realise Alfred was dictating to Tom.

They were only just in time to dodge into the tunnel. It turned out to be a dead end. There was a steel door in front of them and a bloodthirsty gnarl patrol behind them. Finn thought that the unknown danger behind the steel door was better than the known danger of the gnarl patrol. He was entirely wrong. They had blundered into the gnarl guardroom. Some particularly large and unpleasant-looking gnarl were in there. They were armed to the teeth.

In a second, Finn had noticed the fireplace, thrown something into the fire and shouted "Everybody out!"

They didn't need to be told twice. Finn slammed the door and stood with his back to it. His gun was pointed into the darkness, ready for the gnarl patrol if they arrived.

As they waited there was the unmistakeable sound of a gunshot from inside the room. It was muffled by the steel door but they were all keeping very quiet so they heard it.

Then they heard another and another, then what sounded like a volley of shots and the screams of gnarl who were dying behind that door and in no fit state to come out of it.

Then they heard the most unexpected of sounds. Finn was chuckling quietly to himself. His trick of throwing bullets into the fire had worked.

He became silent as they heard the gnarl patrol approach. Three shots from the gun lit up the corridor and Tom launched himself at a gnarl, wielding his knife. The gnarl was more surprised than hurt because Tom was not very good with a knife. The scare was enough however and the patrol retreated again with a further three shots from Uncle Finn to keep them company in the tunnel.

The rearguard and their visitors rushed back to the entry tunnel and Uncle Finn almost pushed the three of them through. As Alfred and Uncle Finn took up position – the position of honour – in the tunnel, the three went a hundred yards down the entry tunnel and then they stopped. They didn't want to leave Uncle Finn and Alfred in the lurch. They didn't want to disobey orders either.

Uncle Finn lay down in the tunnel and got ready to fire his remaining three bullets as soon as Alfred gave the order. He had his knife in his other hand. He reminded himself that he was afraid of nothing.

"Remember you're a Cool. You're cool!" The thought seemed to come from outside himself. It was coming from Alfred and it had all the force of the group mind behind it.

He needed all of his cool when he heard footsteps behind him. Alfred tried to reassure him but messages were not getting through.

"It's me. Black. Ardin is dead. The mission has failed. We must retreat. I am taking over the position of honour and that is an order.

A pitiful handful of the company left through the tunnel with Black in the rear. The rest had found death with honour. Finn tried not to say anything when he heard that. Alfred caught his thoughts and chose not to pass them on. Finn was fearless but he did not welcome death. Finn was mourning for Ardin, such a lovely girl cut down in a war he was beginning to see as senseless.

And what of Luke? He knew the tunnels like the back of his paw of course and he soon came across a cleaning division of gnarlings who were only too pleased to have another pair of paws to help with the work. They talked while they worked. Their talk was all about the big battle which was coming soon. Of course every word they said was shared by the group mind but the chatter of gnarlings was not what he was here for.

He told a story. He had to say a couple of times "No this is not true. It is just something I made up." When the shift was over they were saying that the story had made it seem shorter. That shift repeated the story to other gnarlings and said one of them had just made it up all by himself. It wasn't true. There were no such things as bears and porridge, everybody knew that.

There was a lot of talk about what a naughty girl it was to take their porridge and break Fred bear's playstation.

A lot of them went on to the next stage of making up stories of their own, better stories. If the gnarl noticed anything it was just that the work crews weren't moaning and that was no bad thing.

First one gnarl and then another heard some of the stories. One of them repeated a story at an evening meal. It was all about a gnarl whose head fell off and how he replaced it with the head of a Veck. Those who heard it thought it was a rubbish story although amusing. They were certain they could come up with better stories.

The thirst for stories among the gnarl grew more and more powerful. They were still preparing for the war but in between times they were telling each other sad stories or funny stories and laughing or crying over them.

"You know," one said eventually, "The Gai have stories. Why should they have them and not us? We will defeat them in battle and they will become ours."

They didn't expect what would happen when the day of battle dawned.

The gnarl issued from their tunnels in their thousands. The enemy should be there to meet them. Where were they?

There were only two. One of Ardin's people and one of the Veck. They were unarmed.

To say the gnarl would never kill an unarmed enemy is simply not true. The fact remains that they did not on this occasion. The gnarl approached the pair with curiosity.

"Where are your people? We have come to slaughter them."

"We are surrendering."

As the news spread there was a great yell of triumph from the gnarl. Their war was over in time for the evening meal and all their enemies were now their slaves. There was some disappointment that there was less killing to do but a victory is a victory.

It was a very short time before gnarlings started approaching the slaves and asking to be told stories. Gai was saturated with confidence that thousands of gnarlings would join the group mind and that is what happened.

The gnarl really were awful slave-drivers. It was practically voluntary being a slave to them. They were just pleased with the victory and the fact of having slaves. If one or two, or twenty or thirty or a hundred happened to escape they didn't really notice.

They did notice how happy the gnarlings were. Many of them began to ask if they could share the stories of the group mind of Earth too.

The Ship

The good ship Hiram T Fillbuster was soon ready to depart. Alfred was still part of the group mind of Earth but he was allowed to leave. Gai thought that for him to explore would be the same as the group mind exploring. That made Alfred OK with the idea of going. In any case he couldn't leave the four humans. Who knew what trouble they would get into without him?

Finn took with him a number of bottles of Veck firewater which he had traded for various items in his bag, including his gun. He hadn't said much about the fact that there were only three bullets on earth for that gun. The Veck probably wouldn't need it anyway.

They were sitting round the table drinking tea prior to their launch when Tom talked about something which had been bothering him.

"Uncle Finn. I know the Prof is quite ill. Do you think it is likely he will still be alive when we get back?"

For answer Finn clicked on the video. The Prof had known someone would ask this question. He was sitting in his pyjamas in front of his computer.

"You are worried that I will have kicked the old bucket before you get back. The chances are a million to one. You are travelling above the speed of light. It does strange things to time. You will return, when you return, within five minutes of Earth time from when you left. I will be here to greet you.

"Until then, your five minute mission continues. To seek out new life and new civilisations. To boldly go where no man, boy, girl or dog has gone before."

The End

If you enjoyed this book there are other Space Dog Alfred stories available

The Planet of the Dogs

The Gas Giants

You could also put a comment on facebook or twitter or write a review on Amazon.

Make it a good one!

Derek and Angela

Printed in Great Britain
by Amazon.co.uk, Ltd.,
Marston Gate.